Wool Gathering
A Sheep Family Reunion

poems by Lisa Wheeler • pictures by Frank Ansley

A Richard Jackson Book
Atheneum Books for Young Readers
NEW YORK LONDON TORONTO SYDNEY SINGAPORE

Atheneum Books for Young Readers
An imprint of Simon & Schuster Children's Publishing Division
1230 Avenue of the Americas
New York, New York 10020

The text of this book is set in Cantoria.
The illustrations are rendered in ink and watercolor.

Printed in Hong Kong

1   3   5   7   9   10   8   6   4   2

Library of Congress Cataloging-in-Publication Data
Wheeler, Lisa, 1963–
Wool gathering : a sheep family reunion / written by Lisa Wheeler ; illustrated by Frank Ansley.—1st. ed.
p.   cm.
"A Richard Jackson book."
ISBN 0-689-84369-0
1. Sheep—Juvenile poetry. 2. Children's poetry, American. [1. Sheep—Juvenile poetry. 2. American poetry.]
I. Ansley, Frank, ill. II. Title.
PS3573.H4329 W66 2001
811'.6—dc21   00-061788

For the rest of Mom's flock,
Jack, Gina, Dan, Andy, and Mary.
Watch where you step.
                      —L.W.

For Sierra, for getting us, her parents,
into reading children's books,
a habit we still share.
And Yanni,
our loyal and faithful sheepcat.
                      —F. A.

Wool Gathering

Ewes
and rams
and little lambs,
arrive in buses, trucks, and vans.
They travel far to meet their kin.
Each cousin wears a sheepish grin.
And as the flock begins to gather,
you will see they're really rather
odd, but in a woolly way.
So stay—
each ewe, each ram, each little lambly—
stay and meet this close-knit fambly.

Lambie Kins

Each and every little lambie,
under one year old,
is presented by its family—
welcomed to the fold.

Each lambie gets a gift to keep—
not a one is missed.
Then each is passed from sheep to sheep
and kissed and kissed and kissed!

Odd Ephram

Odd Ephram is the cousin
that no one talks about.
He traded in his woolly coat
and now wears sauerkraut.

Sister Alabaster

Sister Alabaster,
with fleece as white as snow,
is a Kung-Fu master,
excels at Tae Kwon Do,
dabbles in karate,
at judo she is tops.
Just watch your back
'cause she'll attack.
That lamb sure knows her chops!

Aunt Eweginia

Eweginia is a

Ewesful

Ewe. Just wait,

Ewe'll see what she can do. She'll knit

Ewe scarves, she'll knit

Ewe gloves. There's nothing more

Eweginia loves, than knitting white wool

Eweniforms or woolen socks to keep

Ewe warm.

Ewe mustn't watch,

Ewe see, that's rude.

Eweginia knits till she is nude.

Baa-dminton

Can't hit a thing
with our swing.
We aren't all that ambitious.
The net is frayed,
yet we've stayed—
The grass here is delicious!

Brunch

A nibble here

A nibble there

Such tasty vegetation

A nibble now

A nibble then

A yummy celebration

A nibble left

A nibble right

A nibble on the lawn

A nibble here

A nibble there

Where has the infield gone?

Old Ramses

So old   No teeth
So wise   Bad knees
Gray wool   But oh! Oh! OH!
Sharp eyes   What old ram sees!

Hiram's Horns

Our cousin Hiram's horns
grow bigger every year.
So long and wide,
(please stand aside),
they're hard to commandeer.

Balance is quite tricky.
He cannot trot or run.
One careless skip
could make him trip.
He can't have any fun.

But, oh! Those horns are gorgeous!
We simply won't berate them.
We like them fine . . .

. . . come Christmas time,
he lets us decorate them.

Two Wild Cousins

They come from the mountains,
   their wool is unkempt.
Their manners are frightful,
   they come here to tempt
the young and the foolish
   to take up their ways,

tramp off to the backwoods
   to forage and graze.
When we were young lambs
   we were warned by our Granny,
"Beware of your cousins,
   Hill Billy and Nanny!"

Harry

Harry is an ugly ram.
He's got an awkward hoof.
His tail's too long,
his ears too tall,
and his breath smells like a . . .
. . . WOLF!

Little Bo Sheep

Little Bo Sheep

is not too deep.

She's rather dimly witted.

The silly fool,

she blames her wool,

which is too tightly fitted.

Lanolin

Sweet Lanolin
had such soft skin,
she flipped her wool
and grew it in.

Felice

Round Felice
has heavy fleece.
Her wool is big and puffy.
Says Felice,
"I'm not obese!
"Don't call me fat. I'm fluffy!"

Rambunctious

Ewes and rams, both strong and able,
Call the flock and set the table.

Oldsters amble, tails are dragging.
Testy teens are busy bragging.
Little lambies squeal and frolic.
Baby bleaters cry with colic.
Cousins sneak an early snack.
Aunts and uncles yak, yak, yak.

Oats and ivy, sassafras,
Carrots, collards, clover grass,
Fill your bowl then pass, pass, pass.

Chewing, talking, laughing, eating,
Gnawing, drinking, chomping, bleating.
Days like these, sure glad that I'm
Here to share sheep suppertime!

Supersheep

Quiet Cousin Lambert,
mild mannered as can be,
wears nerdy clothes
so no one knows
his true identity.

His secret's safely hidden
inside his tailored vest.
A hero's tool—
he has steel wool!
Beneath a blazing "S."

phone

Itchy

Itchy is a little lamb.
His wool is white as rice.
You wonder how he got his name?
Just ask his fleas and lice.

Uncle Abe Ram

Fussy Uncle Abe Ram
is always neatly shorn.
He manicures each stylish hoof
and polishes each horn.
He tucks a napkin near his chin
and never talks while eating.
Pronouncing every B and A,
enunciates while bleating.
Such a fine appearance,
but no one is impressed.
Though he's neat from horns to feet,
his sheepdog is a mess!

Shear Terror

Drew
grew
her
wool
for
years
and
years
because
she
has
a
fear
of
shears.

Woolverton

Woolverton has a sweetheart.
Her name is Bonnie Nell.
He buys her things,
like diamond rings,
and a golden bell.

Woolverton has a sweetheart.
The only problem now,
is that he's slow,
and doesn't know . . .

. . . she is a dairy cow.

Ewe F. O.

Auntie Gracie had the job
of putting folks to sleep.
Auntie Gracie worked at night—
she was a Counting Sheep.

One night her leap went far and deep
into the galaxy.
She flew away and now is known
as Auntie Gravity.

Sheep Dip

All day they sweat,
their wool gets wet
and bak-ed.
At night they strip
to skinny dip
naked.

Shear Delight

SNIP-SNIP

CLIP-CLIP

BUZZ-BUZZ

NO FUZZ!

Till Next Year

Sun is setting,
sheep are getting
sleepy.

Long good-bying,
ewes are crying,
weepy.

Moon shines brightly,
flock is lightly
snacking.

Lambs are snuggling,
rams are struggling,
packing.

Hugs and kisses, shed a tear
promises to meet next year
as they drive away they hear:

"So long . . . farewool . . . good-baaa."